For Michael, with all my love – C F
For Emily – S M

This edition published by Scholastic Inc.,
557 Broadway; New York, NY 10012,
by arrangement with Little Tiger Press.
SCHOLASTIC and associated logos are trademarks
and/or registered trademarks of Scholastic Inc.
Distributed by Scholastic Canada Ltd; Markham, Ontario

Original edition published in English by Little Tiger Press,
an imprint of Magi Publications, London, England, 2009

ISBN-13: 978-1-84895-013-9
ISBN-10: 1-848-95013-6

Printed in China

2 4 6 8 10 9 7 5 3 1

One Winter's Night

Claire Freedman   Simon Mendez

It was deepest, darkest winter. Wild snow
blizzards had howled through the woods
for days. The animals had been hiding in
their dens, cold and hungry.

But tonight, suddenly, all was quiet and
the sky was clear.

Fox peeked from his snowy den. Out of
the darkness appeared a lone figure,
a badger, gleaming silver in the moonlight.

"Hello," Badger called quietly. "Please, I'm so hungry. Do you have any food to share?"

Fox frowned. He had hardly enough food for himself. But there was such a kind look in Badger's eyes. Fox felt he *had* to help him.

"Wait here," he said.

"Thank you," Badger smiled, gratefully
taking the few berries Fox offered.
Then, Badger went off into the snow,
head bent against the bitter wind.

Mouse was much too cold and hungry to sleep.
As she tossed and turned in her bed, suddenly
she heard footsteps outside. "My, oh my!"
she gasped. "Who's out at this time of night?"

"Hello!" a silvery figure called softly.
"Please, I'm very hungry. Do you have
any spare food?"

   "I've nothing at all!" Mouse grumbled.
"There's no food anywhere!"

   "I understand," Badger nodded,
and he turned to go.

Mouse listened as the heavy crunch of
Badger's footsteps slowly faded. Badger had
seemed so gentle and caring. Yet she had
turned him away.

"Wait!" Mouse scampered after him.
"Hare lives nearby. Maybe she can help!"

Together, Mouse and Badger
struggled to Hare's house.
The wind whipped. Snowflakes
swirled. But somehow, even in
the shadowy dark, Mouse felt
safe beside Badger, his warm
eyes twinkling like bright stars.

Hare was rather angry to be woken up.
And she didn't really want to share the small
handful of berries she'd saved with *anyone*!
"I know it's late, Hare, but I told Badger
you might help," Mouse whispered. "He's
freezing cold and starving. And so am I!"
"I suppose you had both better come in
then," said Hare.

Mouse, Hare, and Badger nibbled on Hare's last few berries.

Hare thought back to when times were much kinder. Then, she and Mouse had spent happy days together, sharing everything. Hare missed those times.

All too soon, Badger thanked them and left. Without him, the burrow felt colder, and the night darker.

"Poor Badger – it's freezing outside!"
Mouse sighed, peering out into the
frosty darkness.
   "I hope he'll be all right,"
Hare said anxiously.
   Just then they spotted a shadowy
figure moving slowly toward them . . . .

"It's Fox!" cried Mouse.

"What are *you* doing here?"
Hare asked him.

"I'm searching for Badger!"
Fox explained. "He was so
exhausted and hungry!"

Mouse and Hare nodded.
They were worried about
Badger, too.

"I think we should go out
and look for him," Mouse said.

In the shimmering snow, Badger's footprints were pools of silver.

The blizzard blew stronger still as the three friends followed Badger's silvery tracks deeper and deeper into the woods.

"Over there!" pointed Fox at last.

There was Badger asleep among the roots
of a tree, covered in a frosting of snow.
"He's frozen!" gasped Mouse. "Poor Badger!"
"We must help him," Fox cried.

Quietly, so they didn't
wake him, Mouse and Hare
gathered some soft mosses
and leaves for Badger's bed.
Fox dug a snowy shelter to
keep him snug.

Then, together they curled up cozy
and warm in their snowy den.
The wind howled and snow fell
thickly, but they had never
slept so well.

The next morning, Badger was gone!
The friends looked around and saw
a trail of silvery footprints stretching
far into the distance.

"I wonder where Badger is going now?" said Fox, "and if he'll ever visit us again?"

But just then, Mouse gave an excited shout. "Look! Over there!"